THE WIND IN THE WALL

HOT
KEY
BOOKS

For Anya, who first loved this story and encouraged me to go further
S. G.

First published in Great Britain in 2019 by
HOT KEY BOOKS

80–81 Wimpole St, London W1G 9RE
www.hotkeybooks.com

A CIP catalogue record for this book is available from the British Library.

ISBN: 9781471404986

also available as an ebook

1 3 5 7 9 10 8 6 4 2

Printed and bound in China

Hot Key Books is an imprint of Bonnier Books UK
www.bonnierbooks.co.uk

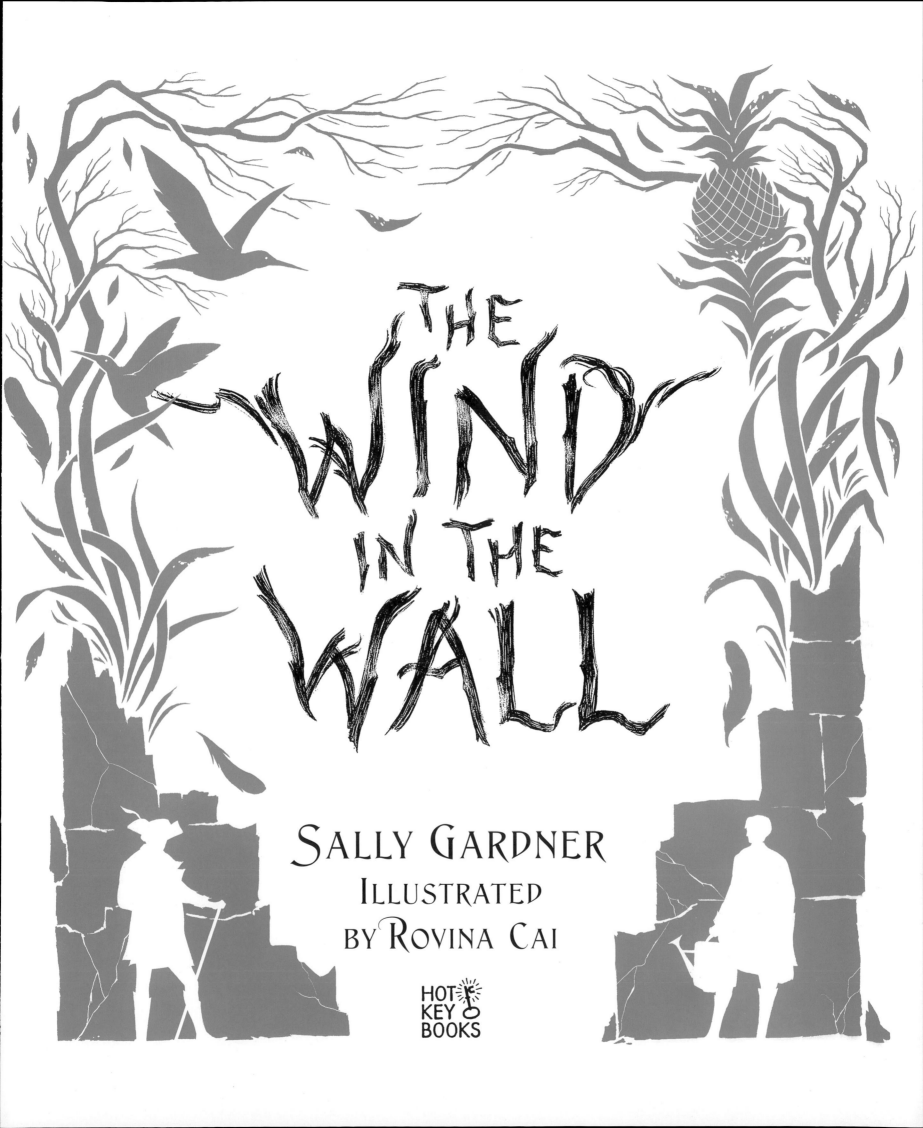

THE WIND IN THE WALL

SALLY GARDNER
ILLUSTRATED
BY ROVINA CAI

HOT
KEY
BOOKS

I have no idea how long I've been incarcerated within these ancient walls. Occasionally, when the stones and mortar are battered by violent winds or beaten by rain I wake up, conscious of my plight. But it is the tapping that has woken me this time.

Tap-tap-tap.

Let me explain how I find myself in this predicament.

I once was a gardener to the Duke of Northumberland. It was our shared passion for the amaryllis that first brought me to the attention of His Grace. We were agreed that in point of beauty few other plants can surpass *Amaryllis belladonna*. I wrote an article about the growing of the flower in a horticultural magazine. I remember it started like this: *To those who possess a small stove . . .*

At that time I believed that, by degrees, I would rise up through the ranks, eventually attaining the position of head gardener. But the duke's admiration for the amaryllis waned and was replaced by a passion for the pineapple. To me the pineapple was a prima donna of acidic fruits, yet all the nobility in England and Scotland had taken up the challenge to produce the finest pineapple specimen in the northern hemisphere, a climate decidedly unfavourable to the growing of this herbaceous perennial. The gardener who possessed the most skill with the sun-obsessed fruit was considered an artisan and in great demand.

Perhaps it was as consolation for the loss of my beloved wife and child to fever that the duke suggested I was put in charge of the pineapple house. Here, in huge plant pots, among a mass of spiky foliage, the monsters grew. It was an honour to be given the job, I know, but – not that I told anyone – I loathed those cursed, scaly dragon eggs. I loathed the heat of the hectic hot-house.

The duke and duchess had taken up residence in Paris. It was said that His Grace astonished the continental nobility by the size of his entourage, the lavishness of his furnishings and by his flamboyant generosity. The fruits of my labours, if successful, were destined to be admired at his dinner table, and even presented to the King of France.

I was permitted to read every book in His Grace's library on the subject of the *Ananas comosus*. I learned that in its native climate, hummingbirds and bats propagate the fruit. But here no such help was to be found and despite all my efforts the pineapples remained small and stunted, refusing to grow in abundance. Those that grew at all tasted bitter, as bitter as the grief I felt for the loss of my child, my sweet wife.

I knew a charlatan when I saw one. His hum had an Irish lilt to it, his eyes were the green of hawthorn, his skin the colour of hazelnut. I felt it to be nothing short of my duty to point out to the head gardener that Mr Amicus was a cheap trickster, the kind you may find in any country fair.

Unfortunately, what I had to say was not taken well. The head gardener told me that Mr Amicus's reputation as a grower of exotic fruit was second to none and that from then on I would be working with flowers. Flowers were the duchess's domain, the head gardener continued, and therefore of lesser consequence than the pineapple. I was undermined, my artistry standing for nothing, and did not speak again about Mr Amicus to anyone.

I began to wonder if it was despair that stunted my efforts with the pineapple, though I was certain that if only I had been allowed once more to grow the amaryllis all would have been well. Perhaps the French king would have delighted in the beauty of the flower, the perfection of its petals, the symmetry of its stem. I had read that in Greek mythology 'amaryllis' was the name given to a shepherdess who shed her own blood to prove her love. Had I not lost my heart when my family died? I believed I had much in common with the amaryllis.

For all my hours of study and the sweat of my work in those heated hot-houses, the pineapples failed. Failure was the one thing the duke would not abide. Such was the severity of his disappointment that I feared I might lose my job and my cottage.

The *tap-tapping* shakes my whole being. Or rather, it shakes the wall and therefore it shakes me. It isn't the wind. The wind is a wheezy breath devoid of speech; it seeps through the crevices, torments one with the possibility of freedom. No, not the wind. I can hear words and, to my parched mind speech is water. But the voices drift off. I long to be washed away in language, not sprinkled with meaningless sentences.

The du[...]
that he[...]
the gro[...]
Mr Am[...]
world a[...]
the Ind[...]
where t[...]
no need[...]

The[...]
a rusty[...]
memory[...]
the exac[...]
I would[...]
my note[...]
Wednes[...]

Mr A[...]
man, pr[...]
were di[...]
hedge. I[...]
and hun[...]

These facts relieved my anxiety somewhat. Surely news of Mr Amicus's outlandish conduct would reach the ears of the head gardener, who would see that I had been proved right: the man was a charlatan.

But alas, no. The first pineapple the wretched Mr Amicus grew was one of the most perfect specimens of its kind. It was reported to the head gardener that His Grace had commissioned an artist in Paris to paint a still life of the cursed dragon egg.

I am the first to admit that every gardener has his secrets.
Just as a magician will perform a trick and never explain the sleight
of hand, the same can be said for gardeners. Nevertheless, I was
determined to find out Mr Amicus's secret, and I doubted that it
would be an honourable one.

From my bedroom window I had seen strange illuminations
inside the pineapple house, sparks of colour glimmering and darting.
My suspicion was that Mr Amicus had brought hummingbirds from
Brazil and kept them in the birdcage. If that was so I wanted to see
them for myself.

It was by the light of a frosty May moon that I went to investigate.
I didn't fear discovery as I knew perfectly well Mr Amicus was slowly
fermenting in beer at the Angel Inn.

Just before dawn she rose to leave, stretching out her feathers. The glory of her wings filled the room with light.

'For the kindness you have shown me I grant you one wish,' she said. 'Use it wisely.'

'Will I see you again?' I asked.

'That is for you to decide,' she said.

Later, when I opened my notebook, I found the feather was missing and felt strangely glad of it.

I was about to go to work when my
cottage door burst open and there he
stood, Mr Amicus, red raw with rage.

'Where is my wife, you interfering
busybody?'

'Gone,' I said.

I backed away the moment I saw
the pistol.

'Then I have come for your heart,
for that alone will bring her back to me.'

There was a flash of gunpowder and
I thought I must be mortally wounded
but to my astonishment, Mr Amicus had
missed. I pushed past him and made
my escape.

When I reached the walled garden I knew I had run myself into a dead end. The wretched man came towards me, a sneer on his face, the pistol cocked, pointing straight at my heart.

Without thinking, I made a wish. Such a pedestrian wish. I have had so long to contemplate all that was then in my power. I could have wished to be with her again but I did not. Without considering my folly I wished that the wall would hide me, and so it did. I felt it softly embrace me, bury me deep within its sandstone folds, mould itself around me.

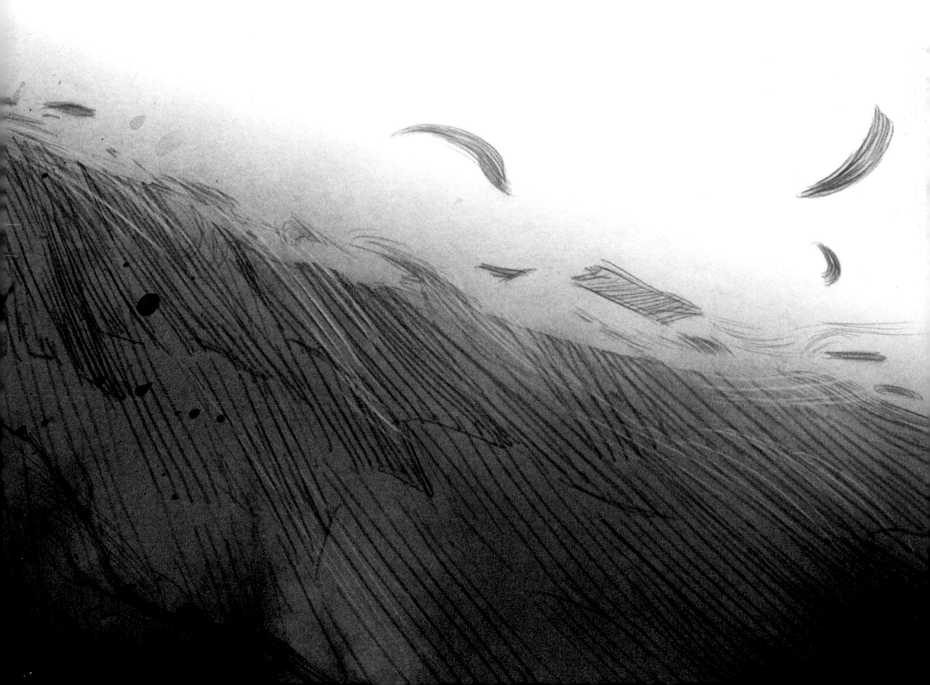